STARK LIBRARY

SUPERSTARS

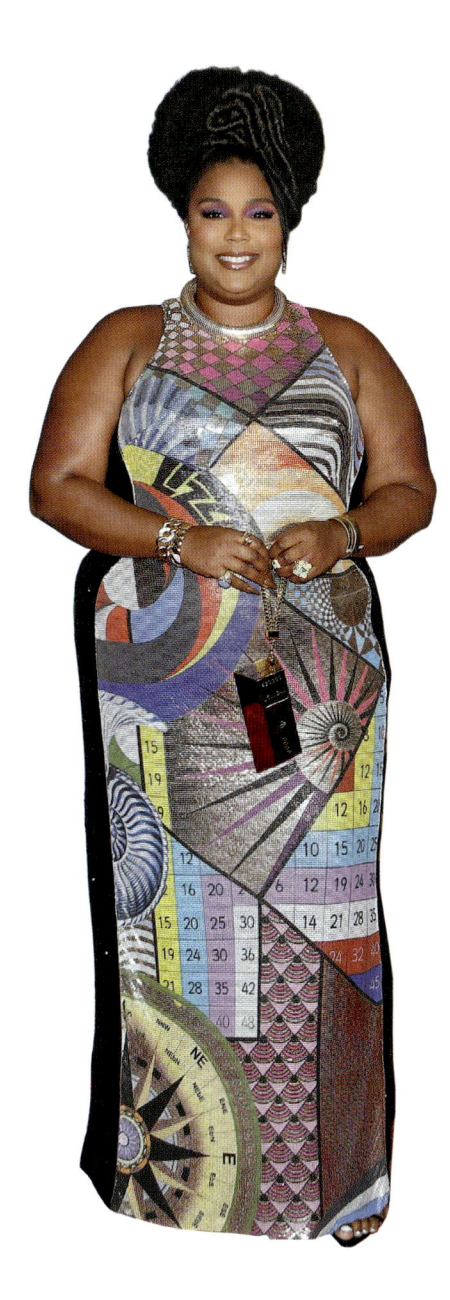

LIZZO

SINGING ★ SUPERSTAR

REBECCA FELIX

Big Buddy Books

An Imprint of Abdo Publishing
abdobooks.com

ABDOBOOKS.COM

Published by Abdo Publishing, a division of ABDO, PO Box 398166, Minneapolis, Minnesota 55439. Copyright © 2022 by Abdo Consulting Group, Inc. International copyrights reserved in all countries. No part of this book may be reproduced in any form without written permission from the publisher. Big Buddy Books™ is a trademark and logo of Abdo Publishing.

Printed in the United States of America, North Mankato, Minnesota

052021
092021

THIS BOOK CONTAINS RECYCLED MATERIALS

Design: Kelly Doudna, Mighty Media, Inc.
Production: Mighty Media, Inc.
Editor: Liz Salzmann
Cover Photograph: Joel C Ryan/AP Images
Interior Photographs: Amy Harris/AP Images, p. 15; Chris O'Meara/AP Images, p. 13; Chris Pizzello/AP Images, pp. 19, 23, 27, 29 (top, bottom right); Dave Starbuck/Geisler-Fotopress/AP Images, p. 9; Gabriele Holtermann-Gorden/AP Images, pp. 25, 29 (bottom left); Joe Abbruscato/Flickr, p. 17; Kevin Mazur/Getty Images, p. 7; Sthanlee B. Mirador/AP Images, pp. 1, 5, 28; Wikimedia Commons, p. 11; Xavier Collin/Image Press Agency/AP Images, p. 21

Library of Congress Control Number: 2020949916

Publisher's Cataloging-in-Publication Data

Names: Felix, Rebecca, author.
Title: Lizzo: singing superstar / by Rebecca Felix
Other title: singing superstar
Description: Minneapolis, Minnesota : Abdo Publishing, 2022 | Series: Superstars | Includes online resources and index.
Identifiers: ISBN 9781532195686 (lib. bdg.) | ISBN 9781098216412 (ebook)
Subjects: LCSH: Lizzo (Melissa Jefferson), 1988- --Juvenile literature. | Rap musicians--United States--Biography--Juvenile literature. | Singers--United States--Biography--Juvenile literature. | Rap (Music)--Juvenile literature. | African American musicians--Juvenile literature.
Classification: DDC 782.42164--dc23

CONTENTS

Lizzo ★★★★★★★★★★★★★★★★★★★★★★★★ 4
Childhood ★★★★★★★★★★★★★★★★★★★★★★ 6
Musical Beginnings ★★★★★★★★★★★★★★★★★ 8
Studies & Struggles ★★★★★★★★★★★★★★★★ 10
Music Recording ★★★★★★★★★★★★★★★★★★ 14
Going Viral ★★★★★★★★★★★★★★★★★★★★★ 18
The Year of Lizzo ★★★★★★★★★★★★★★★★★ 20
Positive Impact ★★★★★★★★★★★★★★★★★★ 24
Timeline ★★★★★★★★★★★★★★★★★★★★★★ 28
Glossary ★★★★★★★★★★★★★★★★★★★★★★ 30
Online Resources ★★★★★★★★★★★★★★★★★ 31
Index ★★★★★★★★★★★★★★★★★★★★★★★★ 32

LIZZO

Lizzo is a singer, rapper, and songwriter. In 2019, she released *Cuz I Love You*. This album made her famous around the world.

Lizzo is also known for encouraging **confidence** and self-love. She believes that self-care is important. Lizzo's **attitude**, songs, and positive messages make her an inspiring superstar!

Lizzo had been making music for many years before *Cuz I Love You* came out.

CHILDHOOD

Lizzo's real name is Melissa Viviane Jefferson. She was born in Detroit, Michigan, on April 27, 1988. She has an older brother and sister. Lizzo's parents are Shari and Michael.

The Jeffersons moved to Texas when Lizzo was nine. They lived in the Houston area. In her fifth-grade band class, Lizzo started learning to play the flute. This became a lifelong passion.

In 2020, Lizzo (*right*) attended the Grammy Awards with her mother.

MUSICAL BEGINNINGS

When she was 14, Lizzo discovered rap and **hip-hop**. These became more musical passions. Soon she began **freestyling**.

Lizzo formed a rap group with some friends. It was called Cornrow Clique. The members wore their hair in cornrows.

Singer Beyoncé was Lizzo's main inspiration. Beyoncé also grew up in Houston.

STUDIES & STRUGGLES

Lizzo started attending the University of Houston in 2005. She studied classical flute performance. However, she dropped out before graduating.

Lizzo joined a band in 2008. But she couldn't afford an apartment. She often slept in her car. Sometimes she slept at the studio where the band practiced.

Lizzo studied flute at the Moores School of Music. It is part of the University of Houston.

In 2010, Lizzo's father died. Around the same time, her band broke up. These events made Lizzo sad and **depressed**. She thought about quitting music.

Lizzo moved to Colorado to live with her mother. A friend who lived in Minneapolis, Minnesota, thought Lizzo would like the music scene there. Lizzo moved to Minneapolis in 2011.

Many famous musicians got their start in Minneapolis. One of them was music superstar Prince.

MUSIC RECORDING

In Minneapolis, Lizzo met Claire de Lune and Sophia Eris. They formed a pop and rap group called the Chalice.

In 2013, Lizzo and Eris formed a new group called GRRRL PRTY. They became known locally for their live performances.

SUPERSTAR ★ SCOOP
Music superstar Prince asked the Chalice to perform on his song "BOYTROUBLE." The song was on his 2014 album, *Plectrumelectrum*.

Sophia Eris often performed as a DJ.

Meanwhile, Lizzo had been working on **solo** music. In 2013, she released her first album, *Lizzobangers*.

In 2015, Lizzo released *Big GRRRL Small World*. This album caught the attention of Atlantic Records. The major music **label** signed Lizzo!

The next year, Atlantic released Lizzo's album *Coconut Oil*. The album saw some success. Lizzo kept writing and recording music. She also performed live shows.

Minneapolis musician Lazerbeak helped Lizzo produce *Lizzobangers*.

GOING VIRAL

In 2018, Lizzo posted a video on the **social media** site Instagram. It showed her performing rapper Kendrick Lamar's song "Big Shot." She also played her flute and danced. The video went **viral**! Lizzo's popularity began to grow.

SUPERSTAR ★ SCOOP
The largest flute store in North America is the Flute Center of New York. Its sales rose 30 percent in 2019. The store called this rise the "Lizzo effect."

⭐ Lizzo named her flute Sasha. It has its own Instagram account, @sashabefluting.

THE YEAR OF LIZZO

Lizzo's next album, *Cuz I Love You*, came out in April 2019. The album received good reviews. But suddenly, a song from 2017 caught people's attention.

Lizzo's song "Truth Hurts" was featured in the 2019 movie *Someone Great*. The song became a hit! It reached number 1 on the *Billboard* Hot 100 chart.

Someone Great stars (*left to right*) Brittany Snow, DeWanda Wise, and Gina Rodriguez.

In November 2019, Lizzo received eight Grammy Award **nominations**. This was more than any other artist that year. Lizzo won three of them.

In 2019, Lizzo also went on a concert tour and appeared in the movie *Hustlers*. In December, *TIME* magazine named Lizzo Entertainer of the Year!

> ... life comes at you fast, and sometimes it can be so hard, but if I can make it, I know you can make it.

—Lizzo addressing fans on Instagram, December 2019

In 2019, Lizzo won Grammys for Pop Solo Performance, Traditional R&B Performance, and Urban Contemporary Album.

POSITIVE IMPACT

Lizzo used to struggle to accept her body. Today, she knows it is part of who she is. Onstage, on **social media**, and in her songs, Lizzo shows **confidence**. She encourages people to see all body types as normal. She hopes her music helps people accept themselves.

SUPERSTAR ★ SCOOP
At the beginning of her live shows, Lizzo asks her fans to repeat a positive statement. It is, "You are beautiful. You can do anything."

Lizzo sometimes repeats her own confident, positive song lyrics to herself as motivation!

In 2020, Lizzo used her fame to encourage people to vote in the US presidential election. Her message was especially aimed at young people. And she promoted **diversity** and acceptance.

Lizzo also said she was recording new music. Her fans eagerly awaited new soulful songs and witty raps from the superstar.

SUPERSTAR ★ SCOOP
In 2019, Lizzo bought a house in Los Angeles, California. It has a recording studio.

"This is my life, and I have to do the best I can with it. And if other people are following it, then I need to make it the best life possible."

In October 2020, Lizzo wore a dress covered in the word "vote" to the *Billboard* Music Awards.

TIMELINE

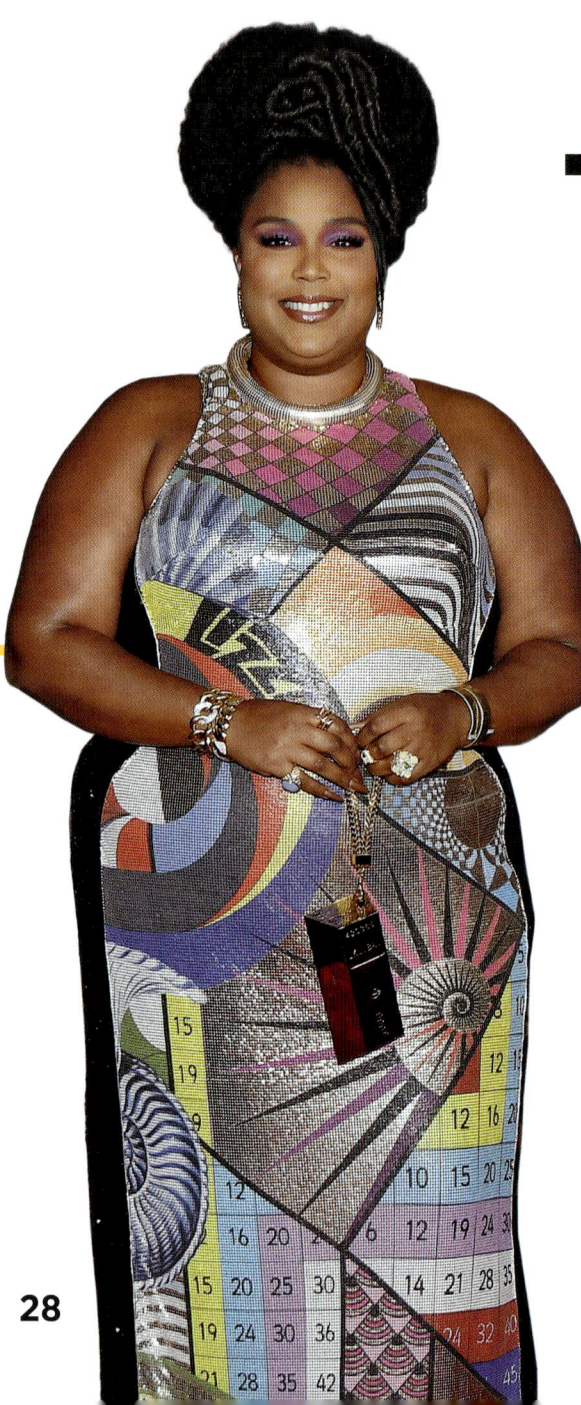

1988
Lizzo was born in Detroit, Michigan, on April 27.

1998
In fifth grade, Lizzo began playing the flute.

2005
Lizzo began studying classical flute at the University of Houston.

2011
Lizzo moved to Minneapolis, Minnesota.

2015 — Lizzo released *Big GRRRL Small World*.

APRIL 2019 — *Cuz I Love You* was released.

DECEMBER 2019 — *TIME* magazine named Lizzo Entertainer of the Year.

2013 — Lizzo's first solo album, *Lizzobangers*, was released.

2016 — Lizzo signed with Atlantic Records. She released *Coconut Oil*.

NOVEMBER 2019 — Lizzo was nominated for eight Grammy Awards. She won three.

29

GLOSSARY

attitude—the way you think or feel about something.

confidence—a feeling of faith in your own abilities.

depressed—feeling sad or dejected.

diversity—having people of different races or cultures.

freestyling—creating rap music in which the words are made up as they are sung rather than having been written ahead of time.

hip-hop—a form of popular music that features rhyme, spoken words, and electronic sounds. It is similar to rap music.

label—a company that produces musical recordings.

nomination—the state of being named as a possible winner.

social media—a form of communication on the Internet where people can share information, messages, and videos. It may include blogs and online groups.

solo—a performance by a single person.

viral—quickly or widely spread, usually by electronic communication.

ONLINE RESOURCES

Booklinks
NONFICTION NETWORK
FREE! ONLINE NONFICTION RESOURCES

To learn more about Lizzo, please visit **abdobooklinks.com** or scan this QR code. These links are routinely monitored and updated to provide the most current information available.

INDEX

activism, 4, 24, 26, 27
Atlantic Records, 16, 29
awards, 7, 22, 23, 27, 29

Beyoncé, 9
Big GRRRL Small World, 16, 29
Billboard Hot 100, 20
birth, 6, 28

California, 26
Chalice, the, 14
childhood, 6, 8, 9
Coconut Oil, 16, 29
Colorado, 12
confidence, 4, 24, 25
Cuz I Love You, 4, 5, 20, 29

de Lune, Claire, 14

education, 6, 10, 11, 28
Eris, Sophia, 14, 15

family, 6, 7, 12
flute, 6, 10, 11, 18, 19, 28

GRRRL PRTY, 14

Hustlers, 22

Lamar, Kendrick, 18
Lazerbeak, 17
Lizzobangers, 16, 17, 29

Michigan, 6, 28
Minnesota, 12, 13, 14, 17, 28

New York, 18

performing, 10, 14, 16, 18, 22, 23
Plectrumelectrum, 14
Prince, 13, 14

social media, 18, 19, 22, 24
Someone Great, 20, 21

Texas, 6, 9
TIME magazine, 22, 29

University of Houston, 10, 11, 28